Georgetown Elementary School
Indian Prairie School District
Aurora, Illinois

TITLE I MATERIALS

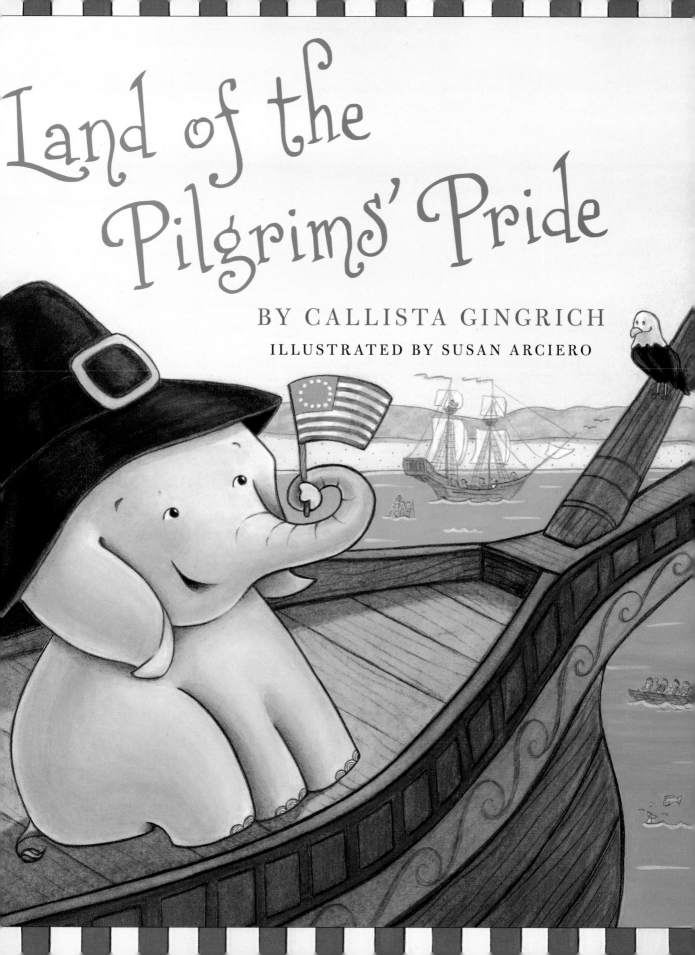

Land of the Pilgrims' Pride

BY CALLISTA GINGRICH

ILLUSTRATED BY SUSAN ARCIERO

★ ★ ★ ★ ★ Acknowledgments ★ ★ ★ ★ ★

Thank you to the remarkable group of dedicated people who made this book possible.

I especially want to thank Susan Arciero, whose beautiful illustrations have once again brought Ellis the Elephant to life.

The team at Regnery Publishing has made writing and publishing *Land of the Pilgrims' Pride* a real pleasure. Special thanks to Marji Ross, Jeff Carneal, Diane Reeves, Cheryl Barnes, and Amanda Larsen for their insightful and creative contributions. Regnery has been remarkable in turning this book into a reality.

My deepest gratitude goes to our staff, including Ross Worthington, Christina Maruna, Bess Kelly, and Woody Hales whose assistance in this project has been invaluable.

Finally, I'd like to thank my husband, Newt. His enthusiasm for Ellis the Elephant and *Land of the Pilgrims' Pride* has been inspirational.

Library of Congress Control Number: 2012946874
ISBN 978-1-59698-829-3
Published in the United States by
Regnery Kids
An imprint of Regnery Publishing, Inc.
One Massachusetts Avenue NW
Washington, DC 20001
www.Regnery.com

Manufactured in the United States of America
10 9 8 7 6 5 4 3 2

Books are available in quantity for promotional or premium use.
Write to Director of Special Sales, Regnery Publishing, Inc., One Massachusetts Avenue NW,
Washington, DC 20001, for information on discounts and terms, or call (202) 216-0600.

Distributed to the trade by
Perseus Distribution
250 West 57th Street
New York, NY 10107

To the brave men and women who came before us
and built the America we love.

★ ★ ★ ★ ★

Ellis the Elephant was a big history fan,
excited to learn how our nation began.
Ellis packed up his trunk and hit liberty's trail—
first stop, Williamsburg, to begin our great tale.

Here he was delighted to see at last
life as it was three centuries past.
Ellis spotted a flag with just thirteen stars,
instead of all fifty as we see on ours.

Ellis was confused, he just had to confess.
"Why thirteen stars—no more and no less?"
"They're for the thirteen colonies!" said his guide in a hat.
"As we ride along, I'll tell you about that."

Our nation's story begins in **Virginia** at Jamestown,
where fortune-seekers from England came to settle down.
But soon in the New World the colonists became aware
that many native people were already living there.

Between the settlers and Indians, conflict quickly arose.
Captain John Smith was soon captured by his foes.
But his young friend Pocahontas courageously stepped in,
saving the Englishman so peace could begin.

Ellis then learned what the King of England did say:
"You may not worship together—freely in your own way."
So the brave Pilgrims set sail across the stormy sea.
They landed in Plymouth, **Massachusetts** and formed a colony.

The Pilgrims agreed that their rules would be fair and just.
With no king, food, or shelter, they had only God to trust.
They wrote the Mayflower Compact for their new colony,
and planted the very first seeds of democracy.

The Pilgrims weren't the only ones from a place far away.
Catholics came from England to live on the Chesapeake Bay.
In **Maryland** the colonists gathered to freely practice their faith,
certain at last they could worship and be safe.

To the north in **New York**, Dutch colonists resided.
Peter Minuit bought Manhattan—land the Indians provided.
Just sixty Dutch coins for the island, all agreed, was a very fair rate!
And they would soon come to find it was prime real estate.

Ellis learned that in America, settlers used what they could find.
Having just arrived from the Old World, they'd left everything behind.
In **New Jersey** cranberries were grown for food, medicine, and dye.
The colonists were resourceful and made the most of a bountiful supply.

In **Connecticut** farmers worked hard to make sure their crops would grow.
Families toiled together through rain, wind, and snow.
Many farmers had cows that provided milk, butter, and cheese.
And Ellis thought it would be great fun to take care of one of these.

In **New Hampshire** the settlers had a very good rule.
Each village in the colony would have its own school.
Ellis thought, "Those kids went to school—just like me!
It's where they all learned reading, math, and history."

But high in the mountains, many challenges remained.
Between the settlers and Indians, friendships were strained.
Fighting between them could sometimes be rough.
And Ellis understood preserving freedom was tough.

On liberty and **Rhode Island**, Roger Williams set his sights,
to make freedom of religion a basic human right.
He believed that the government should not have a say
about the manner in which people could pray.

He met Indians in Providence and learned to speak their tongue,
and soon found they were neighbors he was pleased to live among.
The natives called him "Netop," or "friend," upon meeting.
Ellis smiled and thought, "Now that's a good greeting."

To **Delaware** the Swedish came from far across the sea.
They built homes called log cabins, using wood from sturdy trees.

But here in the New World, there was not a clear plan
for where Delaware ended and Maryland began.
So surveyors Mason and Dixon set out to define
a border we know today as the Mason-Dixon Line!

North Carolina was rugged, a hard place to tame—
a mysterious lost colony its first claim to fame.
Roanoke sadly vanished when, as some say,
hunger and thirst drove the settlers away.

All colonies had their troubles, but some had more than most.
Pirates roamed and plundered along the North Carolina coast.
Ellis learned that one pirate above all others was feared—
he was known far and wide as the despicable Blackbeard.

But there were many honest men who were working at sea.
They shipped goods and supplies like spices and tea.
To **South Carolina** they brought trade of all sorts,
and made Charleston home to a bustling port.

Here merchants shipped crops that the settlers grew,
mainly rice from plantations, and blue indigo, too.
Slaves did much of the work, without freedom or pay—
Ellis knew this cruel practice was not the American way.

Those who needed a second chance came
to the colony of **Georgia** without any shame.
Ellis liked the idea of being a part
of a place where everyone had a fresh start.

The Wesley brothers came to Georgia with a special vision,
to find and welcome people to their spiritual mission.
Their ideas awakened many hearts to living a new way.
And Ellis learned the hymns they wrote are still sung toda

The very last colony on the tour guide's list
was a place that definitely should not be missed!
It's called **Pennsylvania** after its founder, William Penn,
and boasted a great patriot whose name was Benjamin.

Benjamin Franklin was a founding father of our nation,
but his lifelong passion was invention and innovation.
In a storm in Philadelphia he ventured out with kite and key.
When the kite was struck by lightning, he discovered electricity!

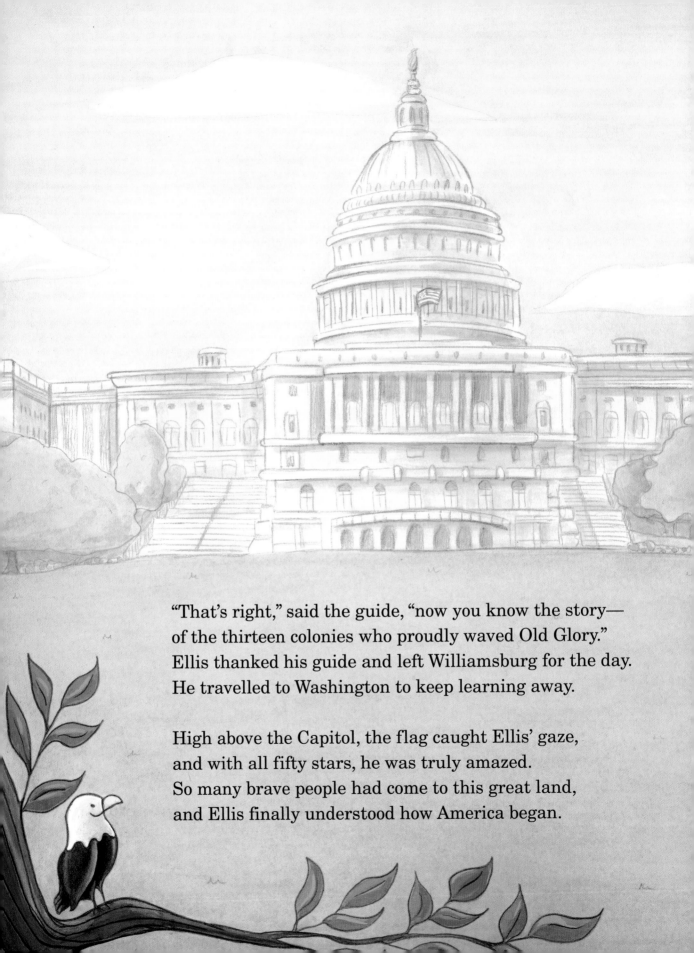

"That's right," said the guide, "now you know the story—
of the thirteen colonies who proudly waved Old Glory."
Ellis thanked his guide and left Williamsburg for the day.
He travelled to Washington to keep learning away.

High above the Capitol, the flag caught Ellis' gaze,
and with all fifty stars, he was truly amazed.
So many brave people had come to this great land,
and Ellis finally understood how America began.

★ ★ ★ ★ ★ Resources ★ ★ ★ ★ ★

Learning so much about the thirteen colonies only made Ellis eager to learn more! Here he shares some of his most interesting discoveries. He was surprised that the first settlers arrived hundreds of years ago! He also found out how much each new colony learned from the ones that came before it. In case you want to embark on your own colonial adventures, Ellis includes lists of historical places to visit in each of the original colonial states.

Virginia: 1607

In December of 1606, three ships—the *Susan Constant*, the *Godspeed*, and the *Discovery*—travelled the Atlantic Ocean from England to find a new home in Virginia. Arriving in the new world with 104 men and boys, these new settlers called their town Jamestown, after King James I of England. Under the guidance of Captain John Smith, the early settlers worked hard and made their town a thriving one. Native Americans such as Pocahontas helped by bringing necessary supplies and materials vital to survive. By 1608 the colony's population had grown to 500 people. However, the winter of 1609, aptly called the "Starving Time," was so fierce that only 60 settlers survived.

Explore the history of colonial Virginia at:

Colonial National Historical Park ★ *A place where 17th century Jamestown comes alive.* ★ *For more information, please visit http://www.nps.gov/colo/index.htm.*

Colonial Williamsburg ★ *This is where Ellis starts his adventure.* ★ *For more information, please visit http://www.history.org.*

Jamestown National Historical Site ★ *This is where it all began.* ★ *For more information, please visit http://www.nps.gov/jame/index.htm.*

Massachusetts: 1620

At odds with the Church of England, Pilgrims set sail across the Atlantic Ocean on the *Mayflower* to start a new life in North America. They originally planned to land in Virginia, but a navigation error led them to current-day Cape Cod. There at Plymouth, they wrote the Mayflower Compact as a set of rules to which they would all adhere. Thanks to the help of Squanto, a native who facilitated communication between the Pilgrims and Massasoit, leader of the local tribe, the Pilgrims were able to survive the brutal winter. The first Thanksgiving was a celebration of the Pilgrims joining with the Native Americans and thanking God for their good fortune.

Explore the history of colonial Massachusetts at:

Pilgrim Memorial State Park ★ *Walk where the first Pilgrims walked when they arrived in the New World.* ★ *For more information, please visit http://www.mass.gov/dcr/parks/southeast/plgm.htm.*

Society of Mayflower Descendants ★ *Find out if you are a descendant of the Pilgrims who first landed on Plymouth Rock.* ★ *For more information, please visit http://www.themayflowersociety.com.*

★ ★ ★ ★ ★ Resources ★ ★ ★ ★ ★

Fun Places to Learn More about the Thirteen Original Colonies

New Hampshire: 1623

In 1623, John Mason, David Thomas, and Edward and Thomas Hilton each received a land grant from King James to settle in New Hampshire. Captain John Smith first called New Hampshire "North Virginia," but King Charles renamed it "New England." It would eventually grow to be a part of Massachusetts. In 1677 it became a separate colony.

Explore the history of colonial New Hampshire at:

Old Man of the Mountain Historic Site ★ *Although this famous landmark collapsed in 2003, it still offers breathtaking views of the New Hampshire landscape.* ★ *For more information, visit http://www.nhstateparks.org/explore/state-parks/old-man-mountain.aspx.*

Maryland: 1634

Fleeing persecution in England, Lord Baltimore (or Sir George Calvert) negotiated with King Charles I to get land located on the Chesapeake Bay. He envisioned Maryland as a haven for Catholics to worship freely. Unfortunately, he died during negotiations, and the second Lord of Baltimore, his son Cecilius, would benefit and help settle the colony in Maryland. Arriving in 1634, they lived in peace with Protestants and got help from local Native Americans. The colony thrived on the Chesapeake Bay.

Explore the history of colonial Maryland at:

St. Clement's Museum ★ *Learn more about Maryland's religious tolerance and separation of church and state.* ★ *For more information, visit http://www.co.saint-marys.md.us/recreate/museums.asp.*

Maryland Historical Society ★ *A starting point for exploring Maryland's colonial history.* ★ *For more information, please visit http://www.mdhs.org.*

Fun Places to Learn More about the Thirteen Original Colonies

Connecticut: 1635

Under the leadership of Thomas Hooker, early settlers from Massachusetts headed to the Connecticut River Valley to farm in more fertile land. Legend has it that their journey took longer than expected, requiring the settlers to subsist on milk from the 160 cows they brought with them. In 1639, representatives from towns in Connecticut drafted the Fundamental Orders, which helped establish a connecting government within their small municipalities. King Charles II in 1662 granted Connecticut colonial status.

Explore the history of colonial Connecticut at:

Henry Whitfield Museum ★ *Tour three floors of priceless 17th–19th-century artifacts.* ★ *For more information, visit http://www.hbgraphics.com/hb/whitfieldmuseum.*

Old State House ★ *This is where the signing of the first constitution in the nation took place.* ★ *For more information, visit http://www.ctosh.org.*

Rhode Island: 1636

Roger Williams arrived in Massachusetts in 1631. Williams soon began to question the legitimacy of the Massachusetts government, specifically some of their religious tenets, and he was banished in 1636. After a long ordeal, Williams bought land from the Narragansett Indians and founded Providence, Rhode Island as a place where all religions would be welcome to practice openly.

Explore the history of colonial Rhode Island at:

Roger Williams National Memorial ★ *Gain a wealth of knowledge on the state's founder.* ★ *For more information, visit http://www.nps.gov/rowi/index.htm.*

★ ★ ★ ★ ★ Resources ★ ★ ★ ★ ★

Fun Places to Learn More about the Thirteen Original Colonies

Delaware: 1638

Ownership of what we call Delaware today changed several times in colonial America. Peter Minuit first settled Delaware in 1624 for the Dutch. Then it was known as New Sweden because the Swedish settled down. Trouble still arose when it came to English lands as Lord Baltimore, the Duke of York, and William Penn all sought to move in. Eventually, the dispute was resolved by surveyors Charles Mason and Jeremiah Dixon, who drew the border that stands today. The colony was eventually renamed after the governor of Jamestown, Lord De La Warr.

Explore the history of colonial Delaware at:

New Castle Court House Museum ★ *Visit the New Castle Court House Museum to learn all about how three counties—New Castle, Kent, and Sussex—declared their independence from the United Kingdom.* ★ *For more information, visit http://www.history.delaware.gov/museum, and http://www.visitdelaware.com/things-to-do/history-heritage.*

North Carolina: 1653

North Carolina was almost the first colony when 100 people from England settled on Roanoke Island in 1587. However, within three years those people who had not already returned to England simply disappeared. It was here that the first American, Virginia Dare, was born on American soil in 1587. This long lost settlement is known today as the Lost Colony.

Later, in 1663, King Charles II granted land to eight men in England—the territory between Virginia and Florida. The new colony was largely settled by outcasts and dissenters from aristocratic Virginia, and by people looking to enjoy broader religious freedoms and the independence of settling small family farms.

Explore the history of colonial North Carolina at:

North Carolina Colonial Trail ★ *Follow the trail to lighthouses, pirates' haunts, and other historical sites.* ★ *For more information, visit http://www.qaronline.org/NCCTrail/NCCT.htm.*

Roanoke Island Festival Park ★ *It's a place "where history comes alive."* ★ *For more information, visit http://roanokeisland.com.*

★ ★ ★ ★ ★ Resources ★ ★ ★ ★ ★

Fun Places to Learn More about the Thirteen Original Colonies

South Carolina: 1663

Considered a part of the "Carolina colony" with North Carolina until 1729, South Carolina's capital city of Charleston eventually became one of the most prosperous ports in the New World. Its founders (eight nobles with a Royal Charter from King Charles) originally hoped to find wealth by growing three expensive products: wine, silk, and olive oil. When the soil and climate proved unsuitable, they found riches in rice, indigo, and tobacco. South Carolina's plantation economy was largely dependent on slave labor, and by 1750 it is estimated that two out of every three people living there were slaves.

Explore the history of colonial South Carolina at:

Boone Hall Plantation ★ *Go back in time to see what everyday life was like on a plantation.* ★ *For more information, visit http://boonehall plantation.com.*

The Charleston Museum ★ *America's first museum, featuring the history of South Carolina.* ★ *For more information, visit http://www.charleston museum.org/home.*

Visit South Carolina ★ *Find out more about colonial South Carolina's historical sites.* ★ *For more information, visit http://www.discoversouthcarolina. com/see-do/history-heritage/default.aspx.*

New Jersey: 1664

King Charles II gave his brother James, Duke of York, the charter for New York. He then mistakenly gave the land known today as New Jersey to Lord John Berkeley and Sir George Carteret. Carteret would name this area New Jersey after the isle of Jersey in the English Channel, where he was born in 1664.

Explore the history of colonial New Jersey at:

Morristown National Historical Park ★ *Visit America's first national historical park.* ★ *For more information, visit http://www.visitnj.org/morris town-national-historical-park.*

William Trent House ★ *Get a sense of colonial family life.* ★ *For more information, visit http:// www.williamtrenthouse.org.*

Visit New Jersey ★ *Explore colonial New Jersey history.* ★ *For more information, visit http://www. visitnj.org/historic.*

★ ★ ★ ★ ★ Resources ★ ★ ★ ★ ★

Fun Places to Learn More about the Thirteen Original Colonies

New York: 1664

New York was founded by Dutch settlers, led by Peter Minuit, who temporarily settled there while they were trading fur in the early 17th century. The settlers called this area New Amsterdam. They lost the land to the British in 1664. King Charles II later gave it to his brother James, the Duke of York. Of course, one of the most enduring stories associated with this colony was the purchase of Manhattan from Native Americans for 60 Dutch gilders.

Explore the history of colonial New York at:

Old Fort Niagara ★ *Starting off as a French fort in 1721, Old Fort Niagara provides a glimpse of the difficulties of defending the Great Lakes region of North America.* ★ *For more information, visit http://oldfortniagara.org.*

Peter Minuit Plaza ★ *At 12:00 every night, the entire plaza is lit with multi-colored lights as a tribute to Peter Minuit, whose name means "midnight."* ★ *For more information, visit http://www.thebattery. org/projects/peter-minuit-plaza.*

Wyckoff Farmhouse Museum ★ *Go back to the early days of Dutch settlers in what is today Brooklyn, New York.* ★ *For more information, visit http:// www.wyckoffassociation.org.*

Pennsylvania: 1682

William Penn was a Quaker who was granted land in 1681 by King Charles II. He would be the sole landowner of Pennsylvania, which translates to "Penn's Wood." Penn would go around Europe to promote Pennsylvania, trying to get people to move there. He was successful, as Pennsylvania would come to welcome people from England, Ireland, and Germany. A little-known fact about Penn is that he lost his fortune settling the colony and spent a year in debtors' prison in England.

Explore the history of colonial Pennsylvania at:

Benjamin Franklin National Memorial ★ *Dedicated to the memory of our first great inventor.* ★ *For more information, visit http://www.nps.gov/ inde/benjamin-franklin-national-memorial.htm.*

Pennsbury Manor ★ *William Penn's home, a living history museum.* ★ *For more information, visit http://www.pennsburymanor.org.*

Colonial Life Museum ★ *For more information, visit http://www.yorkheritage.org.*

Independence National Historical Park ★ *For more information, visit http://www. independencevisitorcenter.com.*

★ ★ ★ ★ ★ Resources ★ ★ ★ ★ ★

Fun Places to Learn More about the Thirteen Original Colonies

Georgia: 1732

Georgia was founded because of the fear that the Spanish would make their way up from Florida and start to create territories in South Carolina. In 1732, King Charles II granted a charter for a new colony to British General James Oglethorpe, who hoped he could attract debtors looking for a new start. Finding it difficult to attract settlers to this new colony, Oglethorpe could not make it flourish, and gave the legitimacy back to the King of England. In 1736, John and Charles Wesley came to Georgia from England on a religious mission.

Explore the history of colonial Georgia at:

Fort Frederica National Monument ★ *See where Georgia's fate was decided in battles between the Spanish and English.* ★ *For more information, visit http://www.nps.gov/fofr/index.htm.*

The Wesley Memorial ★ *The story of John and Charles Wesley is a story of great courage, and they are honored in a beautiful garden.* ★ *For more information, visit http://www.exploresouthern history.com/wesleymemorial.html.*